ANIMORPHS
THE ENCOUNTER

ORPHS
THE ENCOUNTER

K.A. APPLEGATE & **MICHAEL GRANT**
A GRAPHIC NOVEL BY **CHRIS GRINE**

An Imprint of
SCHOLASTIC

For those who look at this red-tail hawk and see
a part of themselves, this one's for you.
–CG

Library of Congress Control Number Available

ISBN 978-1-338-53841-0 (hardcover)
ISBN 978-1-338-53840-3 (paperback)

10 9 8 7 6 5 4 3 2 1   22 23 24 25 26

Printed in China   62
First edition, October 2022
Edited by Zack Clark
Creative Director: Phil Falco
Publisher: David Saylor

DEALIN
HAV
USED VEH

THERE SHE IS.

BEST NOT PECK ME AGAIN, POLLY, OR IT'S THE WRENCH FOR YA.

CLINK

8

1

2

5

CLICK

4

7

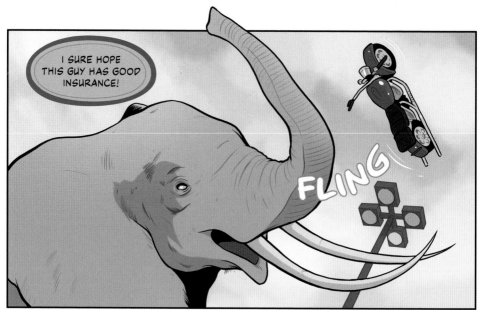

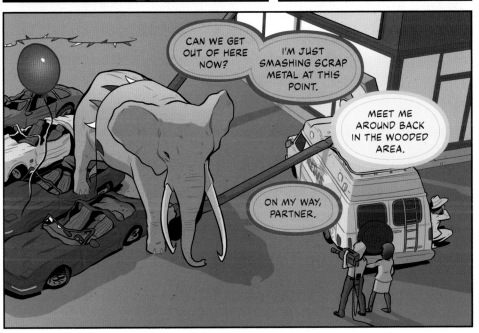

SHLOOOP

CRUNCH

I THINK WE CAN TOTALLY COUNT ON THAT.

IT WAS MY IDEA. I'LL TAKE THE BLAME.

OH, SHUT UP, TOBIAS. STOP BEING ALL NOBLE.

BESIDES, IT WAS AMAZING FUN STOMPING THOSE CARS!

BUT IT WORKED, RIGHT?

THE HAWK GOT AWAY?

SHE DID.

I JUST HOPE SHE FINDS A NICE PATCH OF FOREST NEAR A MEADOW.

THAT'S WHAT WE...THEY LIKE.

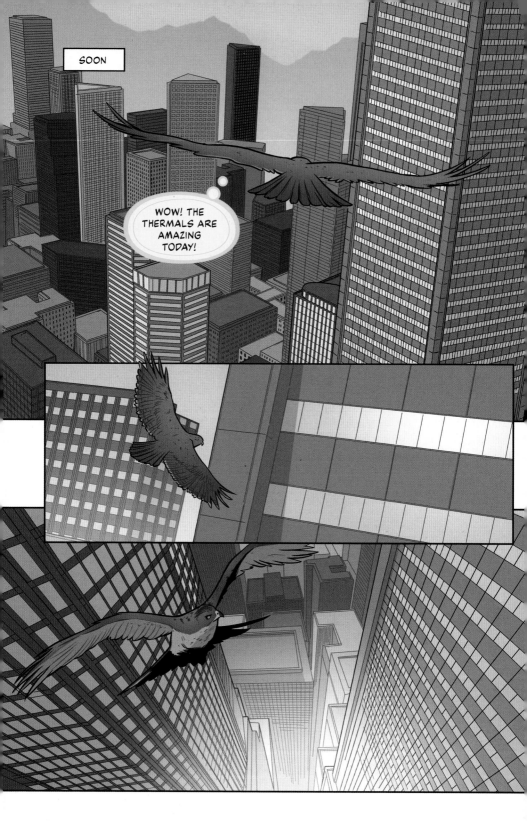

WHOO-
HOO!

WHAT...

19

SORRY WE'RE LATE. WE HAD SOME... UH, STUFF TO DO FIRST.

APPARENTLY, THE OWNER LET HIS INSURANCE LAPSE, SO THAT'S BAD...

STUFF?

ARE YOU TWO OUT OF YOUR MINDS?!

OKAY, MARCO. THAT'S ENOUGH.

THEY PROMISED NOT TO DO ANYTHING LIKE THIS AGAIN, RIGHT, GUYS?

SURE.

OKAY.

WHAT'S YOUR PROBLEM ANYWAY, MARCO?

WE'RE NOT SUPPOSED TO BE RESCUING ANIMALS, RACHEL.

WE'RE SUPPOSED TO BE RESCUING THE ENTIRE HUMAN RACE FROM BEING ENSLAVED BY THE YEERKS.

I THOUGHT YOU DIDN'T WANT TO SAVE THE WORLD, MARCO.

YOU'RE RIGHT.

BUT SINCE ALL OF YOU GUYS THINK YOU HAVE TO SAVE THE WORLD, AND SINCE YOU'RE ALL MY FRIENDS, MORE OR LESS, I FIGURE SOMEONE HAS TO KEEP YOU FROM BEING TOTAL IDIOTS.

25

THEY...JUST CRUMPLED.

THEY JUST FELL IN ITS WAKE.

AND THEN IT FLEW ON TOWARD THE MOUNTAINS COMPLETELY UNCONCERNED WITH THE CARNAGE IT LEFT BEHIND.

BUT THEN WHY WOULD THE YEERKS CARE ABOUT GEESE?

AND THAT'S WHAT THEY WERE. I'M CERTAIN.

WHATEVER IT WAS I SAW...OR DIDN'T SEE...

WAS A YEERK SHIP.

IT WAS A YEERK SHIP.

HOW CAN YOU BE SO SURE?

IT JUST WAS.

I GOT THIS FEELING FROM IT.

ALSO, IT'S UNBELIEVABLY MASSIVE.

FAR BIGGER THAN EVEN THE BIGGEST JET. THIS WAS HUGE.

MORE LIKE A REAL SHIP, YOU KNOW? LIKE AN OCEAN LINER OR SOMETHING.

SO THEN, THE QUESTION IS, WHAT DO WE DO ABOUT IT?

I WANT TO FIND OUT WHAT IT'S DOING.

THE FIRST TIME, I FEEL LIKE IT WAS HEADING AWAY FROM THE MOUNTAINS.

THIS TIME, IT WAS DOING JUST THE OPPOSITE AND IT WAS FLYING TOO LOW TO MAKE IT OVER THE MOUNTAINS.

I'M GUESSING IT'S DOING SOMETHING IN THE MOUNTAINS.

THAT ACTUALLY MAKES SENSE.

REALLY? THAT MAKES SENSE?

HAVE YOU SUBURB-DWELLERS EVER BEEN TO THE MOUNTAINS?

WE'RE TALKING ABOUT A LARGE AREA. NO MATTER HOW BIG THIS SHIP IS, IT COULD HIDE IN A THOUSAND PLACES.

THEN WE'D BETTER START LOOKING RIGHT AWAY.

CASS? WHAT DO YOU THINK?

I HALFWAY FEEL LIKE WE'VE DONE ENOUGH, YOU KNOW?

WE DID EVERYTHING WE COULD FOR TOM.

SO WHY SHOULD WE GET KILLED FOR STRANGERS?

WE CAN'T STAY LUCKY FOREVER. DON'T YOU UNDERSTAND THAT?

SOONER OR LATER, WE'LL SLIP UP.

SOONER OR LATER WE'LL BE STANDING AROUND HERE CRYING BECAUSE ONE OF US...IS GONE.

YOU KNOW SOMETHING?

I'M TIRED OF TRYING TO TALK YOU INTO THIS, MARCO.

YOU WANT OUT? FINE, **YOU'RE OUT!**

RACHEL, BE HONEST. YOU'RE NOT JUST DOING THIS TO SAVE THE HUMAN RACE!

YOU LIKE THE DANGER. THAT'S WHY YOU WENT WITH TOBIAS TO FREE THAT STUPID BIRD.

THAT WASN'T ABOUT SAVING THE WORLD. THAT WAS ABOUT RESCUING SOME HAWK.

I MEAN...
I DIDN'T...

AS OF RIGHT NOW, AS OF TODAY, ONLY ONE OF US HAS BEEN HURT. ME.

BUT I'M NOT GIVING UP. I'M NO LEADER. BUT I'M GOING TO THE MOUNTAINS TOMORROW MORNING.

WHAT THE REST OF YOU DO IS YOUR BUSINESS.

I'LL BE WITH YOU.

YOU SAY YOU'RE NOT A LEADER, BUT I'LL GO WITH YOU.

SAME.

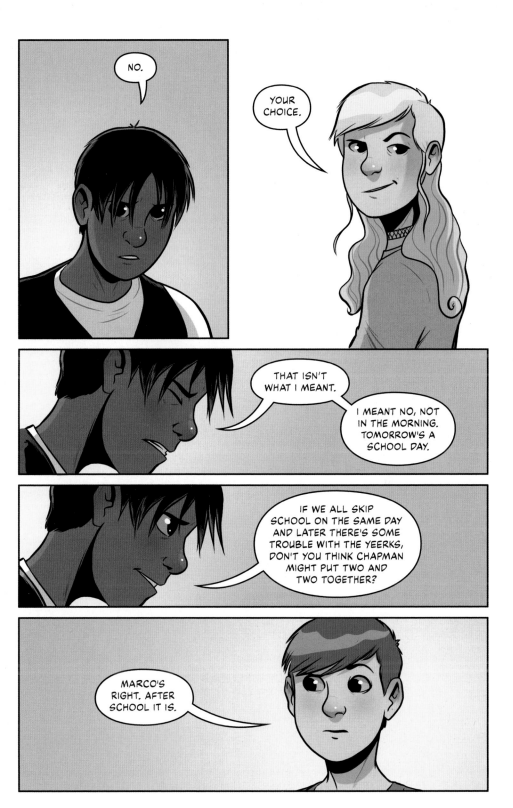

MONDAY

WHY CAN'T WE FLY?

BECAUSE THERE ARE A LOT OF BIRD WATCHERS AROUND.

IT'D BE WEIRD TO SEE US ALL FLYING TOGETHER AS IF WE WERE ON A MISSION.

AND WHAT IF ONE WAS A CONTROLLER?

WE COULD FLY, BUT NO. NO, WE HAVE TO WALK. TWENTY MILES, PROBABLY!

OH, COME ON, MARCO. IT'S AN OPPORTUNITY TO TRY OUT A NEW MORPH!

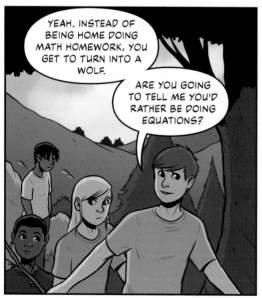

YEAH. INSTEAD OF BEING HOME DOING MATH HOMEWORK, YOU GET TO TURN INTO A WOLF.

ARE YOU GOING TO TELL ME YOU'D RATHER BE DOING EQUATIONS?

LET'S SEE. MATH? OR BECOMING A WOLF AND GOING OFF TO FIND ALIENS?

MAYBE I SHOULD ASK THE SCHOOL COUNSELOR WHAT SHE THINKS?

EVEN IT IT WERE TRUE, I'M CONFIDENT I COULD CONTROL IT.

MARCO, YOU AND JAKE ALREADY FIGHT FOR DOMINANCE, AND YOU'RE JUST ORDINARY GUYS.

SHE'S NOT WRONG.

HEY, WHEN I MORPHED INTO A GORILLA, I HANDLED THAT GORILLA BRAIN OKAY, DIDN'T I?

SURE, MARCO, BUT THAT WAS DIFFERENT.

YOU AND THE GORILLA WERE ALREADY SO MUCH ALIKE.

HILARIOUS.

SLAP

ARE WE DOING THIS, OR WHAT?

HEY, CASS, YOU WANT TO GO FIRST, TO SEE WHAT IT'S LIKE?

SURE, JAKE.

CRUNCH-CH

CRUNCH

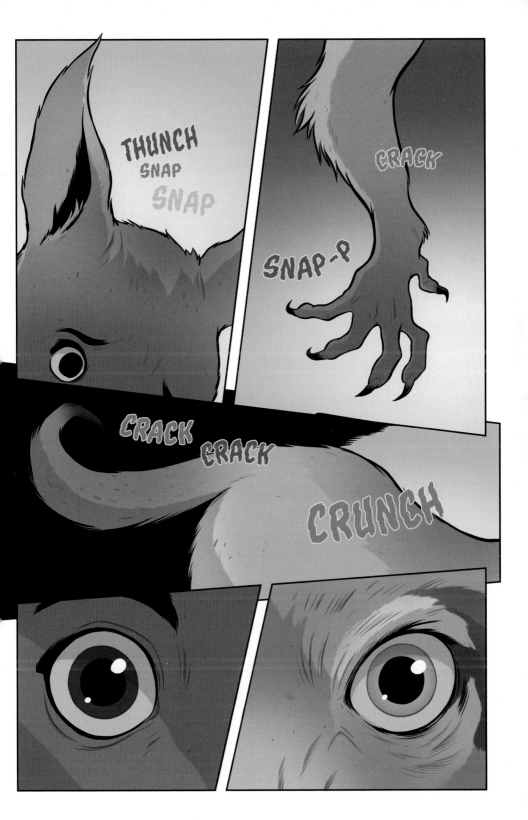

GR-R-R-RRRRR

SOON

47

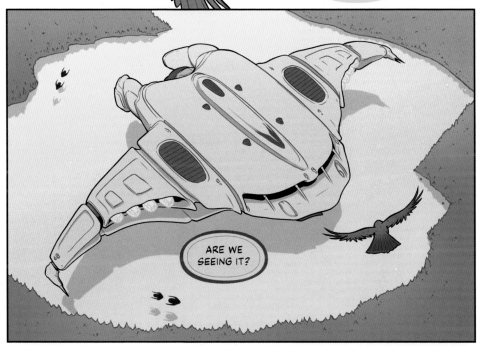

68

69

I'LL CATCH UP IN A FEW MINUTES.

I'M GONNA GO...CHECK ON SOMETHING.

THERE SHE IS.

SHE SEES YOU.

SHE WANTS YOU TO GO TO HER.

YOU BELONG WITH HER.

SHE IS HOME.

YOU SHOULD GO WITH HER.

73

83

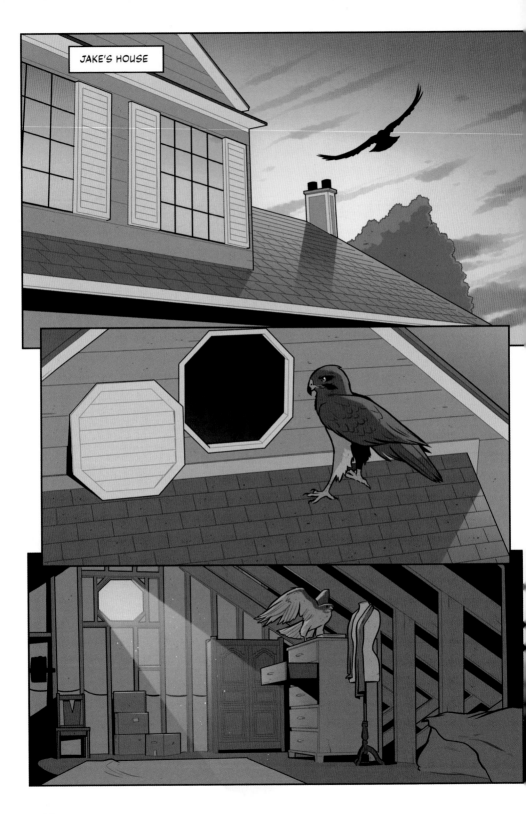

JAKE'S HOUSE

POP

RACHEL'S HOUSE

RACHEL?

TIK TIK

TODAY THE HAWK WE FREED... SHE WAS THERE.

AT THE LAKE. I WANTED TO GO WITH HER. I FELT LIKE I BELONGED WITH HER.

YOU BELONG WITH US.

YOU ARE A HUMAN BEING, TOBIAS.

HOW CAN YOU BE SO SURE?

BECAUSE WHAT COUNTS IS WHAT IS IN YOUR HEAD AND IN YOUR HEART.

A PERSON ISN'T HIS BODY. A PERSON ISN'T WHAT'S ON THE OUTSIDE.

RACHEL... I DON'T EVEN REMEMBER WHAT I LOOKED LIKE.

TUESDAY

93

JAKE'S HOUSE

IT'S ABOUT TIME. WE'VE ALL BEEN WAITING HERE FOR LIKE AN HOUR.

I'M A BUSY BIRD. I LOST TRACK OF TIME.

LET'S MAKE THIS KIND OF QUICK.

I PROMISED TO HELP MY DAD RELEASE A HORNED OWL.

FRIEND OF YOURS, TOBIAS?

WE HAWKS DON'T HANG WITH OWLS.

IF CASSIE HAS TO GET GOING, MAYBE WE BETTER DEAL WITH BUSINESS.

I HAVE TO GET GOING SOON, TOO.

MY GYMNASTICS CLASS IS PUTTING ON AN EXHIBITION AT THE MALL.

OH, I AM THERE!

NO, YOU ARE NOT THERE!

NONE OF YOU ARE GOING NEAR THAT PLACE. YOU KNOW HOW I FEEL ABOUT HAVING TO PUT ON STUPID EXHIBITIONS.

OKAY, WE'VE LEARNED HOW THE YEERKS GET THEIR AIR AND WATER. AND WE EVEN KNOW WHERE THEY DO IT.

AND WE MORE OR LESS KNOW WHEN. THERE OUGHT TO BE SOME WAY FOR US TO USE THIS INFORMATION.

ANY IDEAS?

WHAT?

WHAT WERE YOU GOING TO SAY?

IT'S JUST...

OKAY, LOOK, SO...WHAT IF THAT SHIP DIDN'T GET BLOWN UP OR DISINTEGRATED OR WHATEVER.

WHAT IF IT WAS FLYING OVER THE CITY AND SUDDENLY THE CLOAKING DEVICE WAS TURNED OFF?

HUH...

PEOPLE WOULD PROBABLY NOTICE IT.

OH YEAH, THEY WOULD NOTICE IT.

RADAR WOULD SEE IT, TOO.

A MILLION EYEWITNESSES.

THEY'D NEVER BE ABLE TO COVER IT UP!

PEOPLE WOULD VIDEOTAPE IT.

THEY'D TAKE PICTURES!

THE WHOLE WORLD WOULD SEE.

THE ENTIRE HUMAN RACE WOULD REALIZE WHAT WAS HAPPENING.

AND THEN WE COULD GO TO THE AUTHORITIES.

THEY WOULDN'T BE ABLE TO STOP US! WE COULD TELL ALL WE KNOW!

WE COULD TELL THEM ABOUT THE SHARING.

WE COULD TURN IN CHAPMAN!

I CAN'T BELIEVE I'M EVEN ASKING THIS, BUT HOW DO YOU THINK YOU'RE GOING TO DO THAT?

WE'LL HAVE TO GET INSIDE. WANT TO KNOW HOW?

NOPE.

THROUGH THOSE WATER PIPES.

AS FISH.

JAKE, I JUST TOLD YOU I DIDN'T WANT TO KNOW.

BUT LISTEN, IF WE'RE GOING TO DO THIS MISSION, IT CAN'T BE TILL THE WEEKEND.

WHY?

THE TIMING. WE HAVE TO MORPH TO TRAVEL UP THERE BECAUSE IT'S TOO FAR TO WALK.

EVEN AS WOLVES, THOUGH, IT TAKES TIME. IT TOOK MORE THAN AN HOUR LAST TIME.

IT JUST SEEMED TO ME THAT WE MIGHT WANT TO GET UP THERE IN THE MORNING SO WE'RE READY BY AFTERNOON WHEN THE YEERKS SHOW UP.

THIS TIME WE MAY WANT TO TRAVEL AROUND THAT OTHER WOLF PACK'S TERRITORY.

I DON'T WANT TO GET INTO IT WITH THEM AGAIN.

YOU'RE RIGHT.

SO IF YOU'RE GOING TO CAMP EARLY IN THE DAY, YOU NEED A SATURDAY.

ANYWAY, IT MIGHT BE A GOOD IDEA IF WE HAD AS MUCH INFORMATION ABOUT THE AREA AS WE CAN GET. SO I WAS THINKING--

YEAH. I'LL SCOPE OUT THE SITUATION.

I'LL LOOK FOR SOMEPLACE YOU CAN HIDE.

I HAVE A LOT OF TIME ON MY HANDS.

NO HANDS, EXACTLY, BUT LOTS OF TIME.

SATURDAY IT IS, THEN.

I GOTTA GET GOING OR ELSE I'LL BE LATE.

I FEEL LIKE SOME EXCERCISE. MIGHT GO WALK AROUND THE MALL.

LATER

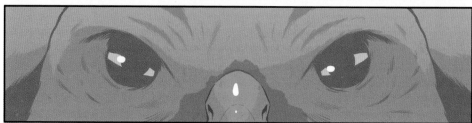

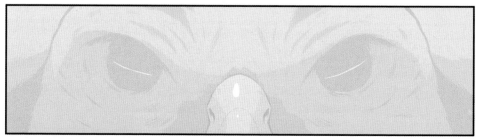

114

115

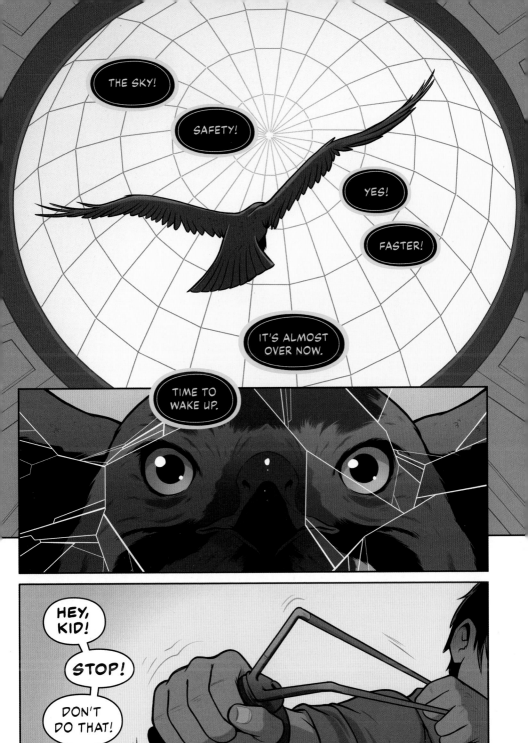

120

I FOUND A PLACE FOR MYSELF.

IT WAS PERFECT RED-TAIL TERRITORY.

A NICE MEADOW SURROUNDED BY TREES. ALTHOUGH THERE WAS ANOTHER RED-TAIL WHO HAD A TERRITORY NEARBY, SO I COULDN'T HUNT THERE OFTEN.

I SPENT MY DAYS HUNTING OR RIDING THE THERMALS.

DAYS WERE EASIER THAN NIGHTS. DURING THE DAY I WAS HUNTING ALMOST ALL THE TIME.

I'D SIT IN A TREE AND WATCH TILL SOME UNWARY CREATURE VENTURED OUT. THEN I'D SWOOP DOWN, SNATCH IT UP, KILL IT. EAT IT WHILE THE BLOOD WAS STILL WARM.

NIGHTS WERE WORSE. I COULDN'T HUNT AT NIGHT.

THE NIGHTS BELONG TO OTHER PREDATORS, MOSTLY THE OWLS.

THE HUMAN IN MY HEAD WAS SAD. LONELY.

THE HUMAN TOBIAS REALLY JUST WANTED TO SLEEP. HE WANTED TO DISAPPEAR AND LET THE HAWK RULE.

HE WANTED TO ACCEPT THAT HE WAS NO LONGER HUMAN.

SUDDENLY I SAW FAST MOVEMENT IN THE WOODS.

A CHASE!

THE PREY WAS RUNNING AWKWARDLY ON ITS TWO LEGS.

RUNNING AND THREADING ITS WAY THROUGH THE UNDERBRUSH.

I COULD HEAR GASPING BREATH. IT WAS WEAKENING. THE PREY WAS SQUEALING. LOUD, YELPING VOCALIZATIONS.

PREY OFTEN SQUEAL.

AND THEN THE WORLD FLIPPED.

HELP!

HELP ME!

SUDDENLY I REALIZED THE PREY WAS A HUMAN BEING.

THE PREDATOR WAS A HORK-BAJIR.

I THOUGHT-SPOKE, YES.

THERE WAS NO ALTERNATIVE.

I COULDN'T LET THEM CATCH HIM. HE HAD SEEN A HORK-BAJIR.

THEY WOULD NEVER HAVE LET HIM LIVE.

BUT NOW HE KNOWS ABOUT YOU! AND HE KNOWS ABOUT THE HORK-BAJIR.

WHAT'S HE GOING TO DO? GO TELL PEOPLE HE WAS CHASED THROUGH THE WOODS BY AN ALIEN MONSTER, AND RESCUED BY A TELEPATHIC BIRD?

GOOD POINT.

BESIDES, IF HE STARTED TALKING OPENLY ABOUT THE YEERKS, THEY'D FIND HIM AND...SILENCE HIM.

EXACTLY WHAT I EXPLAINED TO HIM. I THINK HE'LL PROBABLY KEEP QUIET. HE'LL TRY TO FORGET IT EVER HAPPENED.

YOU SAVED HIM.

I ALMOST DIDN'T. AT FIRST I JUST SAW ANOTHER PREDATOR AND HIS PREY.

NO DIFFERENT FROM WATCHING THE OWLS AT NIGHT.

NO DIFFERENT FROM WHAT I DO MYSELF. KILL TO EAT.

THE YEERKS AND THEIR SLAVES AREN'T KILLING TO EAT. THEY'RE KILLING TO CONTROL AND DOMINATE.

KILLING BECAUSE IT'S THE ONLY WAY YOU CAN EAT, BECAUSE THAT'S THE WAY NATURE DESIGNED YOU, THAT'S ONE THING.

KILLING FOR POWER OR CONTROL IS... EVIL.

I GUESS YOU'RE RIGHT. I HADN'T THOUGHT ABOUT IT THAT WAY.

WHAT YOU DID... EATING...YOU KNOW, WHATEVER. THAT'S NATURAL FOR THE HAWK. RIGHT?

NOTHING A HORK-BAJIR DOES IS NATURAL.

THEY AREN'T EVEN IN CONTROL OF THEIR OWN BODIES OR MINDS. THEY'RE TOOLS OF THE YEERKS.

AND THE YEERKS ONLY WANT POWER.

I KNOW.

YOU ARE HUMAN, TOBIAS.

WE DON'T HAVE TO GO THROUGH WITH THAT.

YES, WE DO. MORE THAN EVER, I UNDERSTAND.

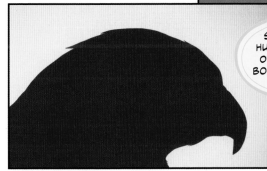

SEE...THERE ARE HUMAN BEINGS ALL OVER, TRAPPED IN BODIES CONTROLLED BY YEERKS.

TRAPPED.

RACHEL, I KNOW HOW THEY FEEL.

MAYBE I CAN'T ESCAPE. MAYBE I AM TRAPPED FOREVER.

BUT IF WE CAN FREE SOME OF THOSE OTHERS.

MAYBE...I DON'T KNOW. MAYBE THAT'S WHAT I NEED TO DO TO STAY HUMAN.

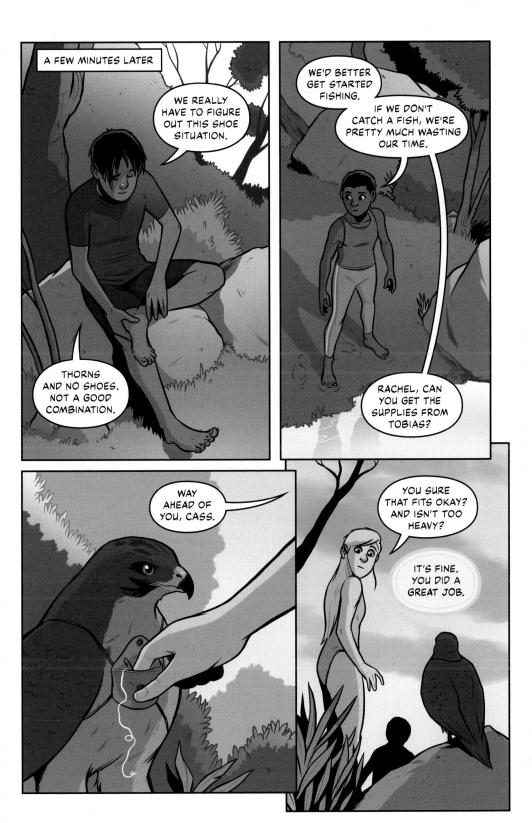

THREE HOURS LATER

THIS IS RIDICULOUS!

WE'RE FOUR-- I MEAN, FIVE--FAIRLY INTELLIGENT HUMAN BEINGS.

AND WE CAN'T OUTSMART ONE FISH THAT PROBABLY HAS AN IQ OF FOUR?

FISHING IS A MATTER OF SKILL AND LUCK.

A SMART FISHERMAN LEARNS NOT TO BECOME FRUSTRATED.

THE YEERKS WILL START ARRIVING IN AN HOUR OR SO.

EVEN IF WE CATCH A FISH NOW, WE WON'T HAVE TIME TO TEST THE MORPH.

YOU REALLY OUGHT TO TEST IT OUT. YOU GUYS ALL KNOW HOW MUCH TROUBLE A MORPH CAN BE AT FIRST.

I DON'T LIKE THIS PLAN.

TOBIAS, YOU WERE IN ON THE PLANNING RIGHT FROM THE START, PAL.

LOOK, DON'T YOU GUYS REALIZE HOW DANGEROUS THIS COULD BE?

I REALIZE. I REALIZE IT PLENTY. BUT I THOUGHT YOU WERE THE BIG, GUNG-HO YEERK KILLER.

SUDDENLY NOW YOU'RE AFRAID?

I'M NOT AFRAID FOR ME.

I'LL BE FLYING AROUND SAFELY WHILE THE FOUR OF YOU GO UP INTO THAT SHIP.

IT'S HARD STANDING BY WHILE SOMEONE ELSE IS RISKING THEIR LIFE. BUT THERE'VE BEEN TIMES WHEN YOU WERE THE ONE TAKING THE RISKS.

LOOK, WE DON'T HAVE TIME TO DEBATE THIS.

WE HAVE A PLAN WE'VE ALL AGREED TO. LET'S GET ON WITH IT BEFORE THE YEERKS SHOW UP.

WE'LL BE OKAY.

I'M GOING UPSTAIRS TO SEE IF ANYONE'S COMING.

BE CAREFUL, TOBIAS.

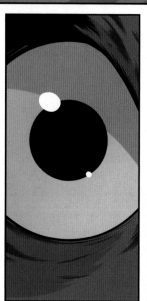

THERE SHE IS.

SHE'S WATCHING ME.

ONLY BECAUSE WE'RE IN HER TERRITORY.

143

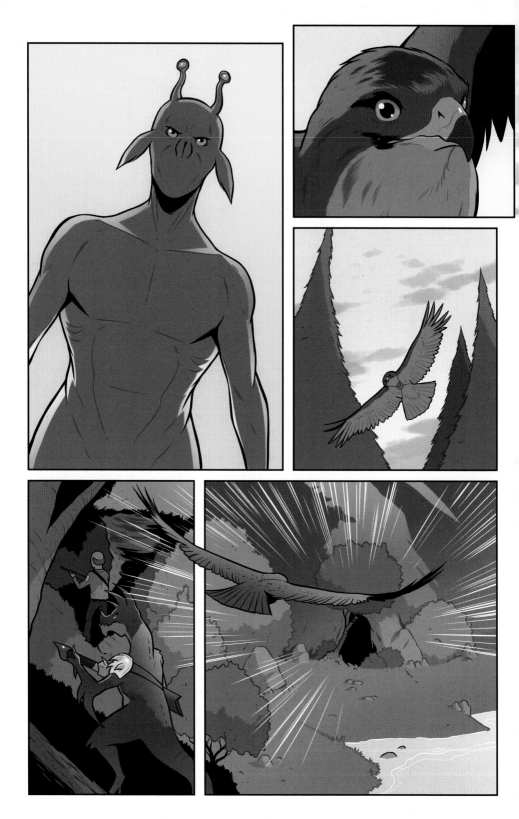

I DISAGREE. I THINK WE SHOULD STILL TRY THIS.

IF WE PULL THIS OFF, IF WE MANAGE TO GET INSIDE THAT SHIP AND DISABLE THE CLOAKING DEVICE WHILE THEY'RE OVER THE CITY... THIS WHOLE THING WILL BE OVER.

WE'VE ALWAYS SAID, IF THERE WAS SOME WAY TO SHOW THE WORLD WHAT WAS HAPPENING... WELL, THIS IS THE WAY.

THIS WOULD BE WAY TOO BIG FOR THE CONTROLLERS TO COVER UP.

EVEN IF THE MAYOR, THE GOVERNOR, AND THE ENTIRE POLICE FORCE WERE CONTROLLERS, THEY COULDN'T HIDE SOMETHING LIKE THIS.

JAKE, YOU'RE NOT LISTENING. I'M TELLING YOU-- THERE IS NO WAY YOU FOUR CAN CRUISE DOWN TO THE LAKE. YOU'LL BE DEAD BEFORE YOU TAKE FIVE STEPS!

ACTUALLY... THERE MAY BE A WAY.

155

SEE, A FISH CAN SURVIVE OUT OF WATER FOR A COUPLE OF MINUTES.

AND THE FISH WE'RE MORPHING IS SMALL.

SMALL ENOUGH FOR...A RED-TAILED HAWK TO CARRY.

EXCUSE ME?

ARE YOU SAYING YOU WANT TO NOT JUST MORPH INTO A FISH, BUT TO MORPH INTO A FISH OUT OF WATER AND THEN BE CARRIED THROUGH THE AIR BY A BIRD?

I'M JUST SAYING IT COULD WORK.

IT **WILL** WORK.

LET'S DO IT!

NO. NO WAY.

YOU GUYS ARE BEING RECKLESS.

NO OFFENSE, BUT THIS RAISES THE DANGER LEVEL WAY BEYOND WHAT IT WAS TO START WITH.

I KNOW IT'S DANGEROUS, TOBIAS.

BUT WE MAY NEVER GET A CHANCE THIS GOOD.

IT WAS MY IDEA.

I'LL GO FIRST.

IF YOU FEEL LIKE YOU'RE SUFFOCATING, YOU HAVE TO BACK OUT OF THE MORPH.

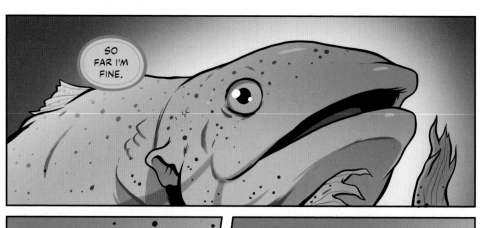

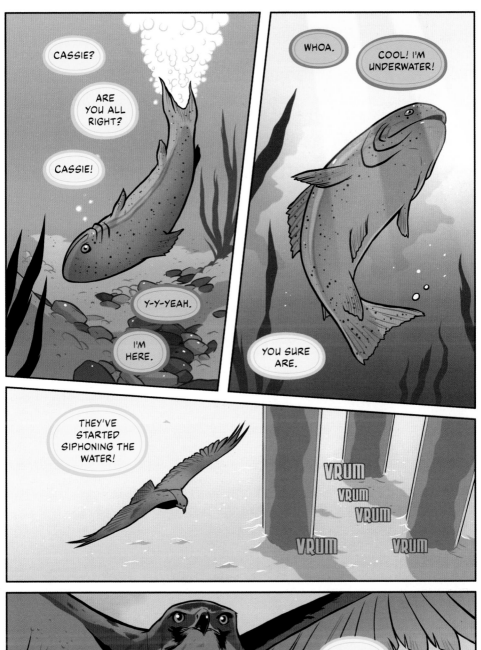

169

174

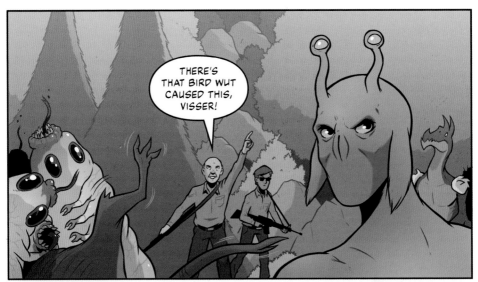

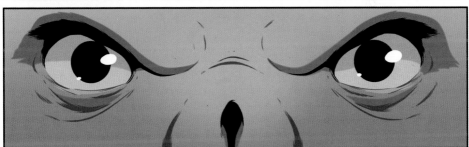

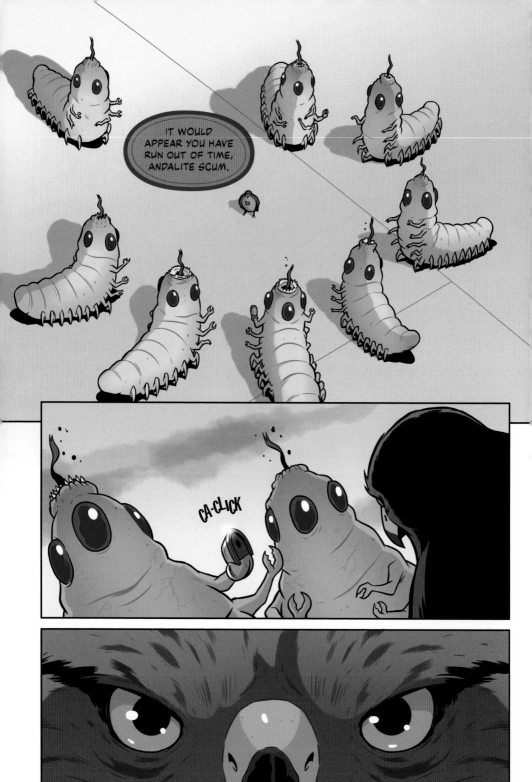

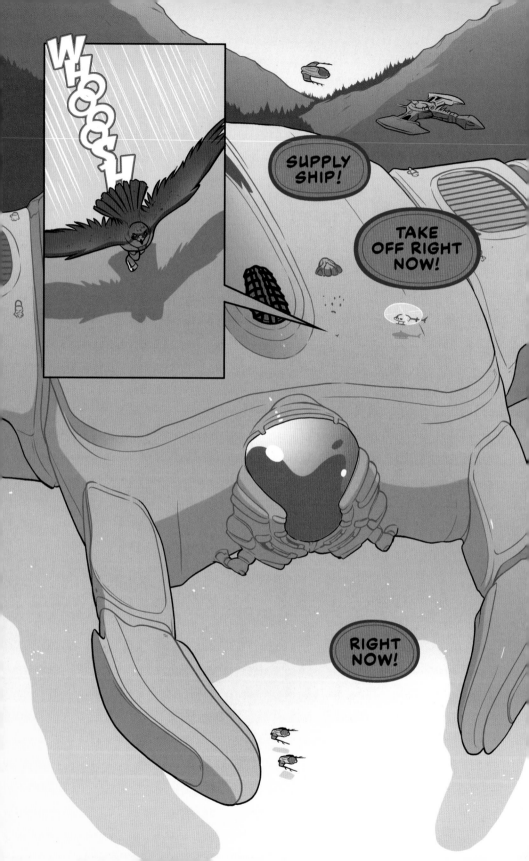

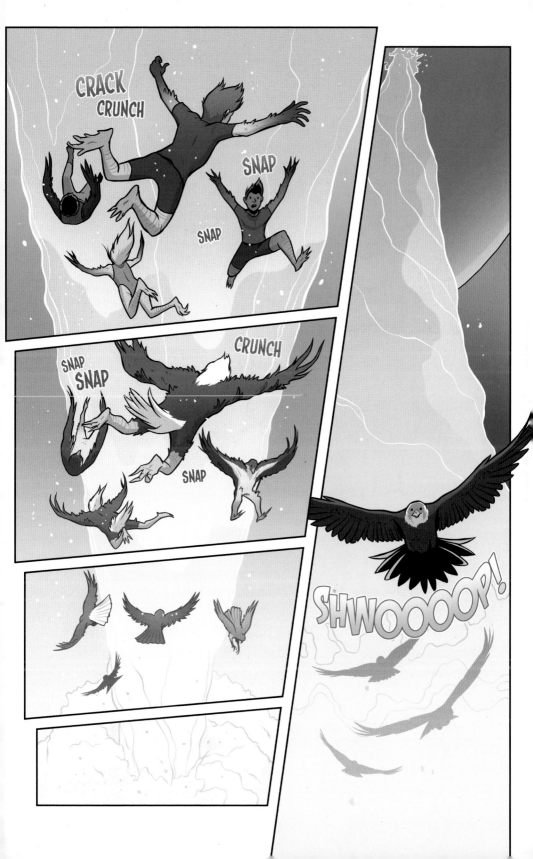

199

SOME STRANGE MIX OF THE TWO.
BE HAPPY FOR ME, AND FOR ALL WHO FLY FREE.

K.A. APPLEGATE is the married writing team Katherine Applegate and Michael Grant. Their Animorphs™ series has sold millions of copies worldwide and alerted the world to the presence of the Yeerks. Katherine is also the author of the Endling series and the Newbery Medal–winning *The One and Only Ivan*. Michael is also the author of the Front Lines and Gone series.

CHRIS GRINE is the creator of Chickenhare and *Time Shifters*. He's been making up stories since he was a kid, and not just to get out of trouble with his parents. Nowadays, Chris spends most of his time writing and illustrating books, drinking lots of coffee, and sleeping as little as possible. He spends his free time with his wife, playing with his kids, watching movies, and collecting action figures (but only the bad guys).

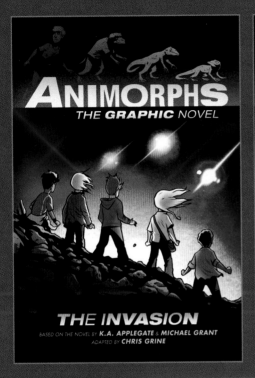

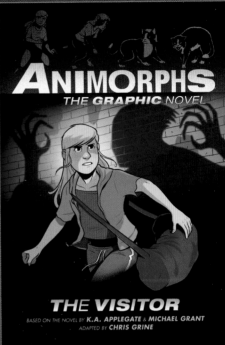

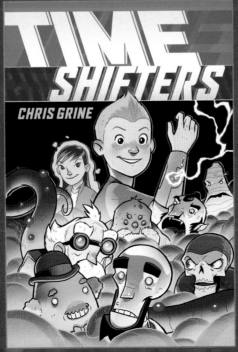